D0771108

ALL EXCEPT AXLE

For Terry and the car guys —S. L. G.

*For my dad, who taught me to drive
and to be unafraid —L. M. W.*

🪔 ALADDIN
An imprint of Simon & Schuster Children's Publishing Division
1230 Avenue of the Americas, New York, New York 10020
First Aladdin hardcover edition September 2020
Text copyright © 2020 by Sue Lowell Gallion
Illustrations copyright © 2020 by Lisa Wiley
All rights reserved, including the right of reproduction in whole or in part in any form.
ALADDIN and related logo are registered trademarks of Simon & Schuster, Inc.
For information about special discounts for bulk purchases,
please contact Simon & Schuster Special Sales at 1-866-506-1949
or business@simonandschuster.com.
The Simon & Schuster Speakers Bureau can bring authors to your live event.
For more information or to book an event contact the Simon & Schuster Speakers Bureau
at 1-866-248-3049 or visit our website at www.simonspeakers.com.
Designed by Tiara Iandiorio
The illustrations for this book were rendered digitally.
The text of this book was set in Avenir Next LT Pro.
Manufactured in China 0620 SCP
10 9 8 7 6 5 4 3 2 1
Library of Congress Control Number 2020931893
ISBN 978-1-5344-4022-7 (hc)
ISBN 978-1-5344-4023-4 (eBook)

ALL EXCEPT AXLE

By **SUE LOWELL GALLION**

Illustrated by **LISA MANUZAK WILEY**

ALADDIN
New York   London   Toronto   Sydney   New Delhi

The car assembly plant hummed with excitement.

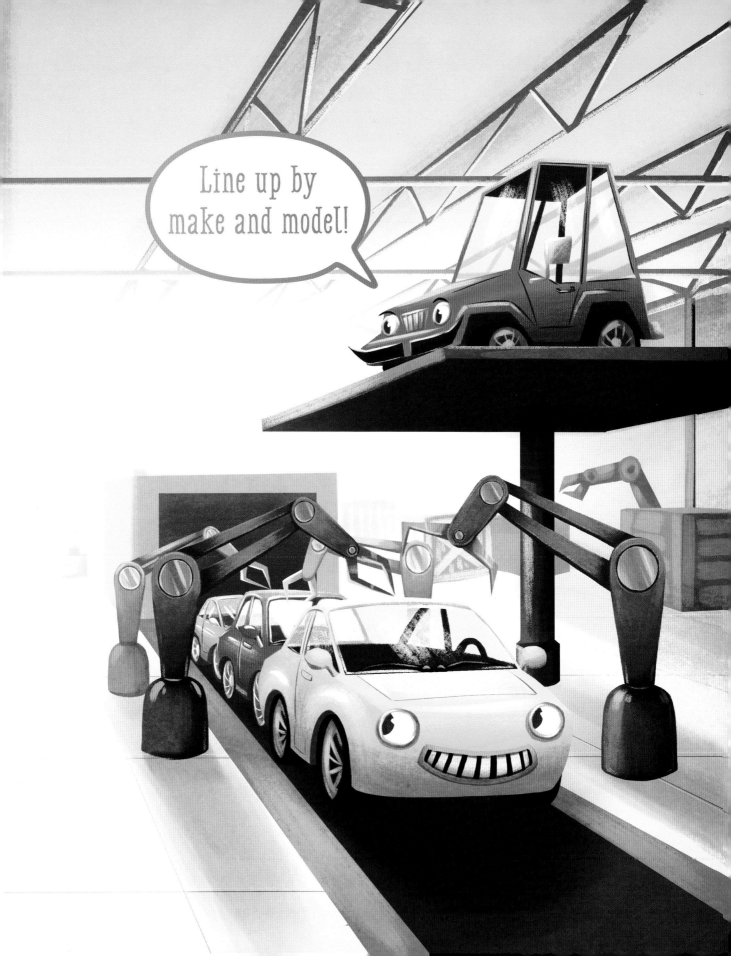

The new cars raced into place.

All except one.

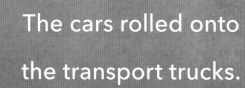

The cars rolled onto the transport trucks.

Axle.

VROOM!

The transport trucks rumbled away.

CITY

All except . . .

Earlene,

and her passengers.

They were waiting for Axle.

Axle coughed.

"I think I'm out of alignment."

"I think you're stalling," said Earlene.

"You can do it, Axle,"

called the other cars.

Axle hesitated. Earlene didn't.

HONNKK!

When they hit the highway, the cars loved the wind on their backs. They leaned into the twists and turns.

All except Axle.

He felt carsick. And worse.

SPLAT!

At the dealership, the cars

couldn't wait to explore.

All except Axle.

He hurried back up Earlene's ramp.

"Let's go back to the plant," he whispered.

"We'll see about that," said Earlene.

VROOM!

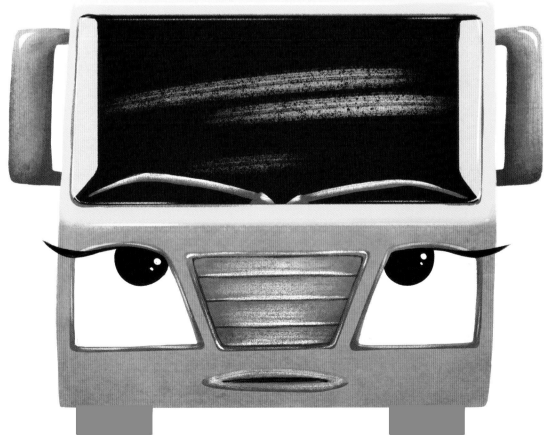

But when they got to the highway, Earlene didn't turn toward the plant. She veered in the other direction.

HONNKK!

TRUCK STOP

"What you need is practice," she said, and pulled off at a truck stop.

Axle crawled down the ramp.

He practiced right turns, left turns, and U-turns.

He slowly circled the truck stop.

"Time for more miles on those tires,"

Earlene said. "Follow me!"

VROOM!

Flatlands.

Axle tried to keep up.

Foothills.

The slope grew

steeper and steeper.

Mountains.

At the top, they stopped to rest.

"Let's stay and enjoy the view," said Axle.

"But, Axle, it's all downhill from here!"

Earlene said with a smile.

Down they drove. Axle trailed far behind.

The road curled and curved.

Suddenly Axle smelled something

burning ahead. "Earlene?"

Earlene rocketed up a runaway truck ramp. Gravel flew.

Oh no! My brakes!

SCREECH!

HISSSSSSS.

RUNAWAY TRUCK RAMP

Axle skidded to a stop.

"I've got a flat! I need help," Earlene sputtered.

The highway was deserted, but Earlene

needed a tow truck. Could Axle continue alone?

As he started back up the mountain,

Axle's engine strained.

His temperature gauge rose.

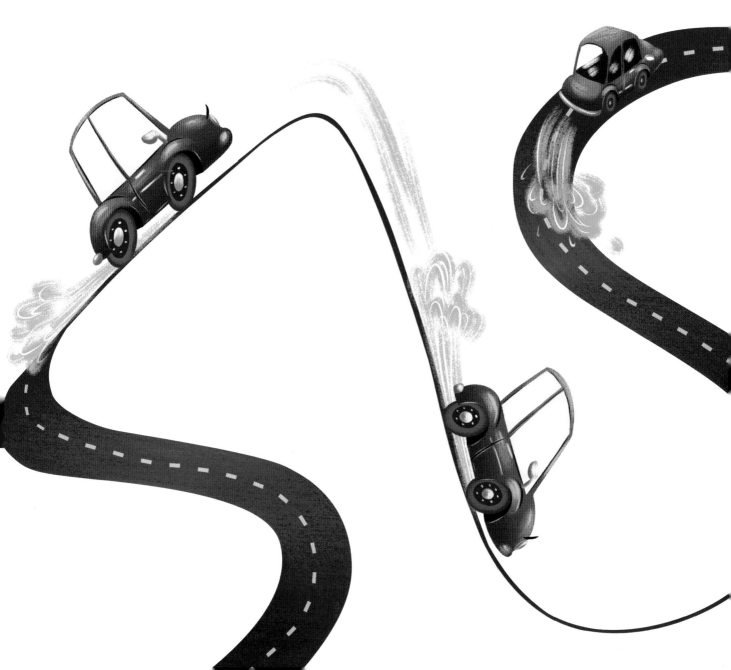

But this time, when he reached
the top, he kept on going!
He raced down, straight to
the truck stop for help.
And . . .

Axle led a tow truck to a grateful Earlene.

"Nice job, kid," the tow truck said. "She needs a new tire, but she'll be fine. Want a ride back to town?"

"Then we'll follow you,"

said Earlene.

The open road called.

Especially for Axle.